Little Bear's New Friend

Little Bear's New Friend
Copyright © 2002 Nelvana
Based on the animated television series Little Bear produced by Nelvana.
™Wild Things Productions
Little Bear characters © 2002 Maurice Sendak
Based on the series of books written by Else Holmelund Minarik and
illustrated by Maurice Sendak
Licensed by Nelvana Marketing Inc.
All rights reserved. Printed in U.S.A.
www.harperchildrens.com

Library of Congress Cataloging-in-Publication Data
Minarik, Else Holmelund.
    Maurice Sendak's Little Bear's new friend / by Else Holmelund Minarik ; pictures by
Heather Green.
        p.   cm. — (Maurice Sendak's Little Bear)
Based on the animated television series, Little Bear; based on the series of books
written by Else Holmelund Minarik and illustrated by Maurice Sendak.
Summary: After Little Bear meets a bear cub living alone by a stream, he and his
friends help the cub find his missing parents.
ISBN 0-06-623817-X — ISBN 0-06-623688-6
[1. Bears—Fiction.   2. Friendship—Fiction.   3. Lost children—Fiction.]   I.
Green, Heather, ill.   II. Title.
PZ7.M652 Mau   2002   [E]—dc21   2001051457

1 2 3 4 5 6 7 8 9 10
❖
First Edition

Little Bear's New Friend

BY ELSE HOLMELUND MINARIK
ILLUSTRATED BY HEATHER GREEN

HarperCollinsPublishers

L ittle Bear came dashing out of the house. He was going camping with Father Bear on Pudding Hill. He was so happy, he just had to run. He ran on all fours halfway around the house, like a wild bear.

When they reached Pudding Hill, Father Bear asked Little
Bear to fetch some water. Little Bear set off for the stream. As
he filled the canteen, he looked up and saw another bear cub
just like himself.

"Who are you?" said the other little cub. "And what are you doing in my stream?"

"I'm Little Bear," said Little Bear. "And how can it be your stream?"

"I live here, so it's my stream," said the cub.

Little Bear was amazed. "So you're a wild bear!" he said.

The cub didn't like this. "I am not a wild bear! I'm just a bear. But I've lived here since I lost my parents in a storm."

"Oh," said Little Bear. "That's really sad!"

Little Bear and the cub looked at each other. They liked each other.
The cub said, "You are Little Bear and I am Cub. You're welcome
here. Let's play."
The two friends splashed and played in the stream.

Little Bear was hiding behind a rock when he felt that someone else was there. He spun around, and there on a rock above him stood a mountain lion. What to do?

Before the mountain lion could move, Cub ran to Little Bear and pulled him along. Together they ran to Father Bear.

After they all had breakfast, Father Bear invited Little Bear's new friend to come home with them. So off they went to Little Bear's house.

When they arrived, Cub was amazed. He had never seen a house before.

That night, Little Bear thought of a way to help Cub find his parents. He said to his new friend, "Tomorrow, Cub, we are going to find your parents. Just you wait and see!"

Cub was smiling as he fell asleep.

The next day, Little Bear gathered his friends and explained the problem to them. Little Bear had a plan. They would all paint pictures of Cub. They would hang the pictures on the trees so that Cub's parents would know that he was near.

They all got to work. Of course, every picture was different. Cub went about looking at the pictures. He was surprised. Did he really look like that?

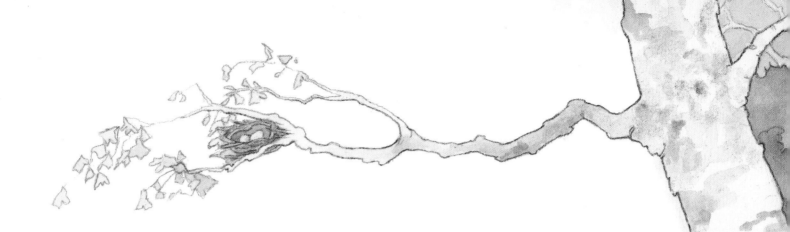

Little Bear, Cub, Hen, Duck, Owl, and Cat hung the pictures on trees by the stream. This was the stream where Little Bear met the mountain lion. That had been scary, very scary indeed.

"What if my parents don't remember me?" asked Cub.

"Impossible!" said Little Bear. "Don't even think of it!" And they all waded into the stream to wash off the paint.

After they finished washing and splashing, Little Bear and
his friends sat down and dried off and waited—and waited.
Duck grew bored swimming in circles.

Soon it came time to check on the signs. But there were no
signs. The signs were gone—each and every one of them. Then
Little Bear saw a robin using a sign to make a nice, warm nest.
The woodland animals had taken the signs!

Cub saw that one last sign was blowing in the breeze.

"Look," he cried, and the animals turned to see the sign land in the water.

Little Bear, Cub, Duck, Hen, Cat, and Owl all jumped into the stream to catch it. The stream was running swiftly now, and the sign and the animals flowed rapidly with the current.

Soon Little Bear, Cub, and Duck were separated from the rest. Down, down they went, down a little waterfall, and landed in a small, safe pool.

Duck was not happy. She said, "First Cub's parents get lost, and then our signs get lost, and now we are lost, too!"

It was growing dark, so Cub led his new friends back to his den, high upon a hillside.

The den seemed strange to Little Bear, who was used to his snug house, but it was dry and leafy and very comfortable. It was a good place for tired little animals to sleep.

When Little Bear saw the valley in the sunlight, he could hardly believe his eyes.

"Isn't it beautiful?" asked Cub.

It was so lovely that words could hardly tell of it.

Duck, Cub, and Little Bear played together in the morning sun. But above the path there was danger, for the mountain lion was watching them, hungrily. As they went by, the mountain lion leaped down and followed them quietly. Oh! Oh, so quietly.

Duck slipped away from Cub and Little Bear and walked
by herself for a moment. Suddenly, she found herself looking
into the eyes of the mountain lion.

When the mountain lion saw Little Bear and Cub, he growled.
Little Bear was very brave. He growled right back.

And then the mountain lion paused. A huge shadow rose
above him. The mountain lion looked up. His eyes widened. He
retreated—very carefully.

There stood a huge bear. Little Bear was surprised and tried
to growl. What else was there to do? Then a big smile came to
Cub's face.

"Father!" cried Cub.

It was Cub's very own father. And there was Cub's mother. She gathered him into her arms. What a loving hug she gave her little lost cub.

Little Bear was introduced to Cub's parents. They were very glad to meet him. It was a joyful time.

"How did you find me?" asked Cub.

Cub's father said, "We found your picture in a nest and knew that you must be near."

But all good things must come to an end. Cub's parents had
to move on—and with them would go Cub.

Little Bear and Cub looked at each other. They had a friendly scuffle—and a big hug. That was good-bye! They knew in their hearts that they would meet again—as all good friends must.

So now the great adventure was over.

At home, Little Bear leaped into Mother Bear's arms.

"My goodness," said Mother Bear, sitting down. "You are getting big!"

Little Bear looked into her eyes. "But not too big," he said.

"No," said Mother Bear. "You will always be my Little Bear!"